Fat Maggie and other stories

EMMA KITTLE-PEY

Patrician Press ● Manningtree

Fat Maggie and other stories

Contents

Emma Kittle-Pey has a MA in Creative Writing from the University of Essex. She writes short stories by night, and teaches Reading Recovery by day at a local primary school. She has two children.

This quirky and subtly witty collection of short stories tackles daily interaction at home, in the workplace, on holiday or at social events.

The animal-related tales contain an interactive element and readers are invited to suggest their own moral at the end of each story, thus allowing them the opportunity to contribute to the dead-pan humour they evoke.

Readers also have a choice about a particular story they wish to read next.

'Emma's stories are spare, in touch with the common world, while having a poetic and witty subtext. Her fiction retains its seeming lightness of tone, but often touches on the moral issues of the everyday and the subtleties of caring and loyalty. You feel that you are in company with a sharp intelligence, which has a calm goodness and a wry humour at its heart' Adrian May

Published by Patrician Press 2013.
For more information: www.patricianpress.com

First published as an e-book by Patrician Press 2013
This edition published by Patrician Press 2013

Copyright © Emma Kittle-Pey 2013

British Library Cataloguing in Publication Data. A catalogue record for this book is available from the British Library.

ISBN 978-0-9927235-3-8

Printed and bound in Peterborough by Printondemand-worldwide

www.patricianpress.com

For Esme and Harvey with love (not squalor)

I would like to thank the original University of Essex workshoppers including Mark Brayley, Katie Ford, Matthew Kroll, and Adrian May for their encouragement with the early stories. Since then, the WriteNighters (you know who you are) for being such a warm and supportive group, and the writers Petra McQueen, Juliet Lockhart and Sue Dawes for their friendship and writerly brilliance. Thank you to Mark and Patricia for getting me going with this, otherwise the stories would still be in the drawer.

Finally, and most of all, I'd like to thank my family, especially my mum and dad, for their eternal positivity and kindness.

Fat Maggie

Hilda the Hyena beams at the assembled group as she approaches the woodland gathering. She lifts her head high and she thinks of the esteem in which she is held here. Her rightful place, she recalls now. Yes, this is where I should be, among these fast creatures. Not nursing sick babies and catching mice for my partner.

'Well well....' says Leonard the Lion. 'Were your ears burning?'

'No, I'm certainly hot but not burning,' she giggles, rubbing one ear against her velvety coat. She can feel the strength in her frame.

'They should have been,' laughs a friendly jackal.

'Yes,' says Leonard the Lion, 'I was just saying what a fine student you once were, the best I had.'

She subtly pushes forward her breast and tilts her head.

'Thank you.' Hilda lowers her eyes. Leonard the Lion continues to talk to the small group surrounding him.

'But have you met Georgia? Now *she* has the right attitude. Have you met her yet, Hilda?'

The lion strokes his mane and, she notices, has a watery eye. 'You should talk to Georgia – now *she* has a good attitude.' Again. 'There she is – with some of the new group.'

So Hilda is introduced to Georgia the Giraffe and Fat Maggie the Hippo.

She giggles and gushes and gapes to Georgia the Giraffe and finally says, 'We are both slick, clever animals! We both love a challenge and a contest! We should get together at the Watering Hole for a drink!'

'Yes, yes of course. I'll contact you,' says Georgia the Giraffe. And then she says, 'Will you excuse me, please?'

Hilda is left with Fat Maggie the Hippo, whom she tries to engage in conversation about the greatness of the jungle. But Maggie can't hear her very well and hasn't got much to say about slickness either so Hilda soon gives up. She says, 'Excuse me, I must go. I have important work to do.' When she turns to leave, she sees Georgia laughing with Leonard.

Hilda reaches the edge of the wood before she drops her head and relaxes her shoulders. Did Georgia use me to get away from Fat Maggie? Does she not realise the depth of my inner beauty, my value as a companion (I'll always laugh at jokes) or the extent of my woodland warrior skills? She is obviously in another league. I wasn't that special after all.

By the time she reaches home, her body is heavy. A baby, the littlest, runs giggling and roly-polying up to her, grabbing a leg so she has to drag him inside.

Harold, her partner, is licking his fur clean and the other babies are curled in a corner. She sits down next to him and he offers her a rat's thigh.

'Thank you, my darling,' she sighs. As she gnaws, she notices a torn and bloody tail resting on his paw. She wipes it gently away.

*

MORAL

Taking what you have for granted will lead you to another place, not always as comfortable.

ANOTHER MORAL

Thinking that you are better than you are, may lead you to lose what you have.

ADD YOUR OWN MORAL TO EMMA'S PAGE ON WWW.PATRICIANPRESS.COM

The Clever Women

Leonard the Lion is sitting looking at the moon. He is wondering where his wife is. She should be home by now. He has a pain in his chest thinking about it.

Then he hears the two lionesses, his wife and her sister, their soft murmurs overlapping one another and the rustling of the leaves through which they are approaching.

He lets them come into view and approach him before he roars, 'Where have you been?!'

'I have been to the Watering Hole with Mary. We have a lot to think about, Mother is very sick.' She goes to the babies and kisses them.

'I have been here alone!' He roars again.

'Yes, I'm sorry, dear. But I really needed to talk to Mary about what we can do to help,' she says with a calm but certain tone. With that she walks back into the foliage from which she came.

Mary is left with the seething lion.

After a few moments of silence she says, 'Let me tell you a story'. And here it is:

Some women and some men lived peacefully together in a green jungle. They liked to bathe in the river. One day the king looked down from his tower and saw them eating and drinking and laughing there. He shouted, 'People, I am hungry, bring me your food.'

The men said to the women, 'We do not want to give him our food, we are hungry too.'

The women said, 'Don't worry, we won't give him our food. We will trick him.' So the women went to the king.

He said, 'You are late. Where is my food?'

'Sorry we are late, your Majesty,' they said. 'We were on our way to give you our food when another king stopped us and said that we must give him our food, as he was hungry.'

'Where is he? I am the king here, not he!' shouted the angry king.

'Follow us,' they said, 'We will take you to the place that we saw him.' They took him into the wood and said – he is in the well, having a swim. The king rushed over to the well and sure enough, when he looked in, he saw another king.

'Why you!' he screeched. 'I'm going to get you!' With that he jumped in after the other king. And, well. That was the end of him.

'You clever women,' said the men and they all carried on bathing in the river.

Mary the Lioness exposes her proud smile to Leonard the Lion who is staring at her. His brow is furrowed and his eyes are piercing. Mary the Lioness thinks, that was a particularly apt story for this situation. I am getting quite good at this. I can see him contemplating that tale. I can see him working out what I meant by it. I really am a very good friend, very good at giving advice. Animals will start saying about me soon, what a good friend, so good at reading situations, at giving advice.

Then Leonard the Lion says, 'Ah. I see the moral of that story. But you didn't tell me it was a story with a moral. I have the morals of an alley cat. I do not wish to hear a story with a moral.'

With that he raises a large paw and rips through her face severing an artery in her neck. And, well. That was the end of her.

*

MORAL

Never think that you are clever enough to advise other people about how to live.

ANOTHER MORAL

Someone that is powerful might not readily acquiesce. Unless they are given, what they believe to be, just cause.

ADD YOUR OWN MORAL TO EMMA'S PAGE ON WWW.PATRICIANPRESS.COM

The Candle Party

Fat Maggie the Hippo holds candle parties. It's her job. She's not very good at just sitting around wallowing in it like the other hippos. She likes to be busy. She wears a smart jacket and she asks friends to hold parties for her. Of course, after that the others want to hold the parties too and that's how she gets her business.

Today she is holding a party at Liz the Leopard's place in the woods. Liz the Leopard is new to the woods and has invited her old friends and new neighbours alike.

When Fat Maggie the Hippo arrives some of the animals are lurking about, others have started to have a drink and mix a little. She is very professional and takes an hour to set up her table of candles. When she has finished it looks like an altar.

She coughs her invitation to come and no-one but Tom the Tortoise (sitting silently nearby) notices. She coughs again.

Her host, Liz the Leopard, and her new friend, Hilda the Hyena have already had a few to drink, and even when Fat Maggie the Hippo gets her attention and tells her that she is ready, the leopard continues to think about serving the nibbles and forgets what she has been told. Eventually Tom the Tortoise has to shout,

'We're ready over here!' And Maggie swiftly moves back to her place by the altar.

The animals come together in a sauntering pack. They sit around her in a semi circular audience.

She holds up her party plan and begins her well rehearsed speech.

'First we'll play a little game so that you can all get to know each other,' she giggles.

She hands a gift bag to Georgia who sits elegantly to the right of her audience. As they pass the bag back and forth she recites an amusing little poem about the nature of her candles, where they have come from, and why they cannot be found elsewhere. Every time she says 'right' or 'left' the animal with the bag must pass it to the right or left. Such a clever little game.

'Excuse me,' says Hilda, 'I hope you don't mind me asking, but how was that supposed to help us get to know each other?' She smirks at Georgia the Giraffe.

Maggie blushes. 'Well it's supposed to help break the ice,' she says.

The hyena glances at her neighbour, flares her nostrils and wrinkles her brow.

Maggie tells her customers all about her candles. She holds them up as she talks and marvels at the length of candle life, and marvels at how her candles won't make black marks on your walls. She shows them her very wide range of candles and tells them what good value they are considering their 'burn life' and considering they cannot be found anywhere else in the jungle.

She talks for a long time. None of the animals speak to each other and only the hyena keeps interrupting her with questions and her opinions on the candles.

'How much is that one?' Hilda the Hyena says. 'Don't you think that's rather a lot for a candle?'

'Well you know these candles have a forty hour burn-time. That is much longer than your standard candle.'

'And what about the black marks you mentioned?' Hilda the Hyena tries to think about black marks on walls but cannot imagine it. 'Do candles make black marks on walls?'

'Oh yes. Terrible black marks. Ruin your décor.'

'Décor?' Hilda the Hyena does not pay much attention to her décor, she is too busy hunting and doing important things.

Fat Maggie thinks that the Hilda the Hyena probably is one of those who do not take much pride in their home. She turns her attention to the other members of the group, who are all sitting silently, politely, giving her their attention, interested in her candles.

Finally she tells them how they can hold a party themselves. How they can get great benefits from holding one, they get a percentage of profits and can buy a certain range of candles at a reduced price for one month. They will not be able to resist.

She rounds off her speech nicely and asks them if they'd like to come and make any purchases or talk to her about having a party themselves.

Hilda the Hyena is raising her eyebrows and her top lip at Georgia the Giraffe, who smiles gently while still looking at the candles.

No one moves.

'I'll just pop to the little girls' room and leave you to chat amongst yourselves.' Fat Maggie leaves them and hopes that they will build up the courage to go and handle the candles in her absence. Another good sales tactic.

When she has gone Hilda says to the jackal sitting next to her, 'Can you believe that? Can you believe it? I cannot believe that. One whole hour she talked. About candles. And about how many hours they burn and how they won't blacken your walls. There are animals starving in the desert and she talks about candles lasting forty hours.'

The jackal bursts into a fit of giggles.

'Oh and the prices. Ridiculous. I can find much better quality candles than that. And I will. You won't catch me shelling out for tat like that,' says Georgia the Giraffe and she delicately synchronises her four legs to stand.

Hilda beams.

The jackal follows Georgia out of the enclosure, her giggles breaking into rapturous laughter.

'Oh,' says Liz the Leopard. 'Yes. Well, you know, I didn't want to have a party at all but she just kept going on and on at me until I said I would. Really, I'm not into candles myself I have more important things to worry about.'

'Yes,' said Hilda. 'Like animals starving in the desert. Honestly. And she tells me that I will not find a longer serving candle. I think she must be mad.'

When Fat Maggie returns they've all gone, apart from Liz the Leopard, who is tidying up. 'Where are your friends?' She says.

'Gone,' says Liz the Leopard. 'They've gone to carry on drinking at the Watering Hole.'

'And did they want to place any orders, hold any parties?'

'No. I'm afraid not.'

'Oh. Well I'm afraid that you're not entitled to your hostess gift or your discount on the tiger print range for the month of October. BUT, not to worry, you *are* entitled to this voucher which enables you to receive a ten per cent discount on anything in the catalogue.'

'Thank you,' says Liz the Leopard, looking a little downhearted about this, Maggie thinks. 'I'll leave you to clear away your things.'

Fat Maggie puts the candles back carefully into position in the black candle holder, a special case she was allowed to purchase after holding ten parties. And one of which she is very proud. Funny lot, she thinks. No sales at all. Sometimes they're just unpredictable old things, customers.

She can't understand it. She'd have leapt on those candles if she'd never heard about them before. In fact that's what she did. And she couldn't believe her luck when she heard she could work with them too, become a party planner herself.

She smiles as she places the last of the candles in the case.

There.

Perfect.

*

MORAL
Don't expect others to reach your high standards, particularly where candles, and home décor are concerned. ADD YOUR OWN MORAL TO EMMA'S PAGE ON WWW.PATRICIANPRESS.COM

This Charming Lion

Leonard the Lion's face breaks into a smile. He knows that with that smile the room will glow, that the parents at the back will give him their full attention, will shush their babies. And that the new students at the front will gaze upwards, enthralled by his enthusiasm.

He swizzles and swirls, points line by line at the college anthem, sings in a loud and frankly theatrical manner, all the while creating a performance worth watching.

The other teachers sit around the edge, backs straight. Watching. Some singing, some mouthing the words, all smiling. They too forgive him when they saw the shiny white teeth, glistening in the morning sun. Who could remain angry with such a charmer? What a credit to the college he is. And such a family man. Four little kiddies and he's always off home early to help out his wife. She's a lucky lioness.

At the end of assembly he is called in to see Petra the Puma, who after congratulating him on another fine performance, asks him if he will, this year, be helping her by taking the students on a field trip to the desert.

'You know I'd love to,' he says. 'But I have to get home to help with my own kids.'

His eyes drop to the floor. 'My wife, you know, she really can't cope on her own.'

'Yes,' says Petra the Puma. 'I know you do your best.'

'And, of course, I do the evening classes as well.'

'I know, you do enough. Too much. I'll ask Belinda instead. She's always willing to help.'

When he gets home the children are eating their tea and his wife smiles and offers to make him a drink. She carries on feeding and clearing up while he drinks his drink.

'Will you give them their bath in the river tonight?' She says quietly.

'I'm very tired,' he says. 'You know how tired I am. I work hard all day and when I get home I need a rest.'

'Right,' she says. When she brings them back from their bath, he is in the kitchen.

'Look at the state of this floor,' he says. 'There's a raisin on it.' And then he clatters about doing the drying up and making sure she knows all about it.

That night the littlest is suffering with a cough and she gets up to give their son drinks on several occasions. In the morning she does not wake, and Leonard the Lion decides that he will have to get up when one of the others call. As he does so, he phones his mother.

'Oh yes I'm up with the babies.' He says.

'Oh, daaarrrrlinngg! And you've been working hard all week. You must be tired!'

'Yes, well,' he says. 'She's in bed, isn't she. Again.' His mother can hear the babies in the background. She feels her chest crunch with anger.

Later that day, the elderly lioness, Leonard the Lion's mother, Magda, is at the Watering Hole with her friend Hilary.

'I don't know what happened,' she said. 'I brought up such wonderful, helpful children and they've all ended up with such lazy good-for-nothings.'

*

MORAL

Don't always believe what you hear, or see.

ADD YOUR OWN MORAL TO EMMA'S PAGE ON

WWW.PATRICIANPRESS.COM

The Home for Sick Animals

Hannah the Hyena is an involuntary resident of the home for sick animals. She is allowed to leave her room in the morning, and she is not allowed back into it until it is bed time. This is because she will lie in her bed all day long if she stays in her room. And why shouldn't she? Why should she follow their rules? They say things and they tell her lies.

One day the nurse asked her what her favourite food was. She told her that it was berry pie even though that was only her favourite food at that moment, not all of the time. The nurse told her that if she took her medication, which she did, the next day she would bring her some berry pie. But she never did.

Today she is sitting in the communal lounge when a nurse comes to tell her she has a visitor. It's Georgia the Giraffe. That shiny do-gooder. Here she comes.

'Well – have you got anything for me? An orange. Thanks. Right come and sit in here.' Georgia comes in and sits down in the communal room with all the other animals.

Tilda the Tiger raises her head and starts to talk to Georgia but Hannah is not going to let her. She's *her* visitor.

'Sorry to talk to your visitor,' she says quietly as Hannah the Hyena snarls at her.

A walrus in the corner is talking about knives and drugs and Nazis and Georgia the Giraffe is fidgeting in her chair.

Hannah the Hyena doesn't notice. She's thinking, 'What is he talking about? Is he talking about me?'

She stands up and walks over. 'What do you mean? What's a Nazi? Oh, lovely.'

She walks back, 'Where are my cigarettes?'

Hannah the Hyena looks around the stones. 'I can't find them.'

She tells Georgia the Giraffe to move. Then she thinks, 'I shouldn't have done that. She might not come again'.

'Sorry,' she says.

Georgia is getting up to leave.

She says she'll come again next week.

The following week, Hannah waits for Georgia and hopes that she will have a visitor, but she doesn't come.

Then one day along pops Fat Maggie the Hippo. She comes in to see Hannah, because she heard from her mother that Hannah the Hyena had had some troubles. She plonks herself down in the room with the other animals.

'Have you brought me anything?' says Hannah the Hyena.

'No sorry, I haven't. Is there anything you would like?'

'Um. Well, I like rats.'

'Oh, I don't think I can catch rats. They're too fast for me.'

'I like cigarettes.'

'Oh I don't know where to get those.'

'You can get them from Clare.'

'Oh. I'm not sure about that.'

'Oh, never mind.' Hannah the Hyena stuffs her paws under her body and then reshuffles herself and stretches out on the ground.

Her eyelids are dropping and Fat Maggie the Hippo is not sure what to do. So she sits next to Hannah the Hyena for a long time while she sleeps, and listens to Tilda the Tiger talk about her husband who is going to bring her a hot water bottle.

A few moments later, Tilda the Tiger darts her eyes toward Fat Maggie the Hippo and says, 'It's awfully hot in here wouldn't you say?'

Fat Maggie the Hippo jumps as Hannah the Hyena shouts, 'You're always saying how hot you are! So why is your husband bringing you a hot water bottle?'

None of the animals reply, but Wayne the Walrus says, 'There is a full moon tonight. Do you think they'll come out tonight?'

'Well, I will,' says Hannah the Hyena, 'I'm going out to use the new cigarette lighter.'

Fat Maggie the Hippo rolls onto her side and then onto her feet. 'I'll go now then,' she says.

'Yes,' says Hannah. 'Thank you for coming.'

'I'll come again.'

'Right,' says Hannah the Hyena and she wanders off to use the new, expensive but safe, cigarette lighter that the inmates are allowed to use to light their cigarettes.

The next week, at the same time, Fat Maggie the Hippo knocks on the hospital door again.

*

MORAL

Some people are more dependable than others.

ADD YOUR OWN MORAL TO EMMA'S PAGE ON

WWW.PATRICIANPRESS.COM

Laura

Laura the Lioness visited the doctor, and sniffled to him that she couldn't stop crying. He said, after some explanation of her daily existence and worries that she couldn't put her finger on, that she needed a rest.

At this point she managed another burst of tears and said, 'Oh, thank you, thanks.'

He ushered her out of the room to where Marion the receptionist stood frankly, and where he whispered in Marion's ear that Laura the Lioness needed a week at the home for sick animals. Marion looked at her and nodded, and immediately Laura the Lioness felt smaller and looked after.

Leonard the Lion was the first to pet and soothe her, and tell her to sit where she was, while he packed her bags. He said that it would be good for her, and that she needed to get better. Meanwhile, he would ask his mother to come and look after the babies. Laura the Lioness was too tired to resist.

When she got to the hospital, the nurse welcomed her and Leonard the Lion was the picture of concern as he carried her bag into the small room.

'There, my darling,' he said, 'you stay here and rest. Everything will be taken care of.'

He took out her things and put them on the small dresser, while she sat down on the bed. There was no light in the small room but Laura the Lioness did not mind.

When Leonard the Lion left, the nurse saw the poor lion bury his head in his paws.

She sighed for him, and said to Laura the Lioness, 'Come along and meet some of the others.' So Laura the Lioness followed her into the communal sitting area.

She saw Hannah the Hyena, whom she hadn't seen for a number of years. She'd known her when they were all young. The hyena sisters, Hilda and Hannah, had been in and out of their lair before they moved to the other side of the jungle. Before she'd got together with Leonard. Hannah the Hyena had been a beautiful and admired creature, slick and fast with a firm breast as she had grown.

One day, she'd seen Hannah the Hyena at the Watering Hole. Hannah the Hyena, having drunk too much whisky, was swinging herself around a tall bamboo. She grasped the smooth stem with the crook of her elbow, and in her paw she held a bottle. Around and around she swung, alternating elbows, wriggling her bottom and her shoulders, and then grabbing the tree tightly with her eyes shut as though it were a lover, or a child, or someone loved. She swung away from the tree, staring at it, releasing it, and waved the bottle in the air before she stumbled backward into the lake.

Laura the Lioness remembered standing staring at the spectacle. She remembered that they did not rush to save her from the lake, but that when she emerged spluttering and spitting water, they walked on by their heads held high, noses in the air. Later, they talked for hours about what they had seen.

And then a few years on they'd seen Hannah the Hyena again, although this time she'd been in the hospital and she had a vacant look in her eyes. You could see her bones through her matted fur. Laura the Lioness had cringed at the sight of her, and had hidden behind the Leonard the Lion. 'That's what happens,' he had said.

This time, she followed the nurse and sat on the opposite side of the room to Hannah the Hyena. She looked around the room at the other animals and she thought, 'What am I doing in a place like this? I don't belong here!' And she began to cry again.

Some of the animals looked at her. 'There there,' they said. 'Not to worry. We won't bite.' She peered through the tears and saw Hannah the Hyena, who was rolling a cigarette.

'Want one, Laura?' said Hannah the Hyena. Laura the Lioness hadn't been called Laura since she was a young lion.

'No, I don't,' she said.

'Suit yourself,' said Hannah the Hyena and she went outside.

Laura the Lioness looked at the animals on either side. There was Wayne the Walrus who had smoked and drunk too much since he'd been a boy. And there was Tilda the Tiger who looked down at herself.

'You're in the room next to me,' said Tilda the Tiger, who kept her head down low as she spoke.

'Yes. For this week,' she sniffled.

Tilda the Tiger didn't look at her but kept her chin to her neck.

Hannah returned.

'Who's taken my orange?' She shouted, and started to search frantically under the cushions where she had sat, and then near the surrounding animals.

Some of them looked at her.

Some of them carried on their own conversation and ignored her.

Then she looked up at Wayne the Walrus who was talking, and said, 'What are you talking about? Are you talking about me?'

Laura the Lioness sat in the communal lounge for half an hour. She had never heard conversation like that before. It seemed random. It seemed disconnected. It seemed that everyone said what they thought the moment it entered their heads. She was a little scared but her body would not allow her to move.

Soon it was bedtime, and the nurse came and told the animals that they had five minutes. They got up and walked outdoors. She thought she'd follow, but Tilda the Tiger, sitting next to her, said, 'Last cigarette.'

The next day Laura the Lioness didn't want to leave her room. But the nurse came and said, 'You have to get up dear.'

So she got up and went to the communal lounge and sat again and listened to animals saying strange things. Hannah the Hyena told the nurse that she knew what she was up to, and the nurse said, 'That's enough of that or there'll be no pudding for you.'

'Pudding! Ha! That pile of shit you regurgitate! Call *that* pudding?'

Laura the Lioness looked at Tilda the Tiger who was burying her chin further into her neck. Wayne was laughing. 'No pudding for *her* now,' he nodded at the Laura the Lioness.

That evening Leonard the Lion came to visit her. He said that he didn't want to alarm the children, so he hadn't brought them with him. They sat in her room and he said, 'How is it?'

'Strange,' she said. 'They're like children in here. They get treated like children.'

'Well, they need looking after,' he said. 'They're not normal.'

'Well, why am I here?' She asked.

'To make you better,' he said.

'What's wrong with me?' She asked.

'We're not sure are we, dear?' He said, 'Try not to worry, it will make you ill.'

As they left the room and he asked if she needed anything, they walked down the corridor and Hannah the Hyena was in the entrance to the communal lounge.

'I know you,' she said.

'I don't think you do,' he said.

'I know you, I saw you. You clawed Mary. And then you ate her. I saw you. I was in the tree.'

'She doesn't know what she's talking about,' he said. 'She's mad.'

His wife followed him down the corridor. Fat Maggie the Hippo tried to open the door to come in, and Leonard the Lion pushed past her.

'You can't stay in here,' he said to his wife. 'I'm going to take you home.'

'I have to stay,' she said. 'I'm here for a week. I need to get better, remember.'

'No, you won't get better in here,' he said. 'This isn't the kind of place you need. I'll be coming to collect you tomorrow.'

*

MORAL

Always treat people with respect because you never know what you might learn.

ANOTHER MORAL

People that unguardedly speak their mind are, perhaps, the most honest of us all.

ADD YOUR OWN MORAL TO EMMA'S PAGE ON WWW.PATRICIANPRESS.COM

Hilda

It was odd that they should meet there. On holiday.

Laura the Lioness looked at Hilda the Hyena and said 'Hilda?'

And Hilda the Hyena, who recognised her instantly, apart from the luminescent scar that ran like lightening from her ear to her breast, said, 'Laura?'

They hadn't seen each other for what seemed like a lifetime. Laura the Lioness did not waste time telling Hilda the Hyena everything that had happened in her life since they had last seen each other – her marriage, her babies, Mary, the bloody divorce.

Hilda was with her husband. She was a little embarrassed that she didn't have that much to tell. Everything had been pretty much normal for them.

Then Laura the Lioness asked about her sister, Hannah the Hyena. Hilda the Hyena said, 'Yes she lives near our mother. Our mother looks after her.'

'What happened to her? I met her at the home for sick animals once,' said Laura the Lioness sadly, 'and I remember when she was such a talented, normal child.'

Hilda the Hyena looked at her blankly. Hilda the Hyena could not remember her sister as a talented, normal child. She only knew what she had become now, and she had forgotten the rest, and most of the time she liked to forget that she had a sister.

But Laura the Lioness said, 'Don't you remember when we had midnight feasts? Don't you remember doing shows and concerts, and she played the violin and spoke with those funny accents?'

Hilda looked at her blankly and said, 'No. I don't remember.'

In bed that night Hilda thought how odd it was that she couldn't remember. She could not remember the things that Laura the Lioness had said, but they must have been true because the Laura the Lioness had said them.

That night she had a dream, this was how it was:

The children were lying together on the floor. It was Christmas morning. One of the adults was filming them opening their gifts.

By the sides of them lay the remains of the gnawed midnight feast.

The children weren't really being filmed opening their presents. They were being filmed opening their presents for a TV show they were doing about secret agents and someone stealing the presents from under the tree.

There was Hannah speaking in a silly accent, and Hilda was posing in front of the camera. Later in the dream, they were doing a proper show and Hannah was playing the violin and Hilda was introducing all the acts.

Then Hilda sang a song, which was nice because she had a child's voice. But when Hannah sang, it was like hearing the voice of an angel.

When she woke up she remembered the dream and it was one of those dreams that you remember as well as if you had seen a film.

She remembered that her sister had been beautiful and intelligent and creative. She looked back and she thought, 'Was it that she could not cope with reality? Or could reality not cope with her?'

That day she goes to visit her mother, and her sister. When she arrives she is surprised to see Fat Maggie the Hippo sitting in the front room.

'Hello,' she says. 'What are you doing here?'

'Oh, me? I come by every week and take Hannah out to the shops, or for a drink of water, or whatever she fancies really.' Fat Maggie the Hippo smiled. 'I didn't realise you were related,' she continued, 'but I should have guessed.'

Hilda the Hyena said, 'Yes, I haven't been around much. But I plan to come now.'

'Lovely,' said Fat Maggie the Hippo. 'Maybe we can all go out together.'

'Perfect,' said Hilda the Hyena.

*

MORAL

If good things come from where you least expected, then maybe you weren't looking in the right place.

ADD YOUR OWN MORAL TO EMMA'S PAGE ON
WWW.PATRICIANPRESS.COM

Living with Grandma

Mum was going through a tough time. Divorcing my dad and with two girls to look after. It played havoc with her nerves, or so she says. That's how I ended up with Grandma, and Grandpa. At first for a while, and then for good. We lived in a bungalow on St.John's, two bedrooms, not a great deal of space.

As I grew so did the washing pile. One day my grandmother made a new rule. 'You can only put washing in the bin on Tuesdays and Thursdays. No other day of the week. Is that clear?'

'Yes, Grandma.' I was not really bothered about the rule. It made no difference to me. I just accepted her ways, and put my washing in the bin on Tuesday and Thursday. Sometimes I had to think about which day of the week it was and return to my room with an armful of washing. I hid it in the bottom of my wardrobe, until it was a washing day. Sometimes I forgot and the pile in my wardrobe grew, too big to put in all in one go, so it had to be shared out amongst the next few washing days.

It was early one Sunday morning when I realised that Johnny Ashton was going to be at school with the boys' school band, on Monday, and that all of a sudden it was important that I wore my best blouse.

'No washing until Tuesday!' My grandmother barked, 'you know the rules!' I took the blouse back to my room and began to sweat when I thought of seeing Johnny Ashton whilst wearing the other one, particularly as I'd be on show at the piano. As I sat on my wobbly bed, on the itchy Welsh blanket, and leant back against the wall, through the window I saw my grandmother talking to Mike Freeman whilst pruning her roses in the front garden.

I took my chance and crept over the plastic floor rug in the kitchen to the cupboard where she kept the washing powder and took a cupful, locking myself in the bathroom with it. Pleased as punch, I washed the blouse myself in the warm water of the avocado sink, enjoying the silky transparent cotton sliding over my hands.

I rinsed and wrung the blouse, rolled it up and put it in my bag for church. It was the only thing I could think of to do. As my grandparents conversed with Pru Richards and Angela Stanton at the entrance, I wandered innocently around the back to where the sun shone on the grave of Harvey March. It dried my blouse nicely while we sang 'One More Step' and took our communion. When I went to pay my respects to Great Aunt Jeannie, I marvelled at the crisp white blouse and thanked Mr March while I was at it.

And so along with the fabric of my teenage existence came a mission to clean and dry without being caught. The rules of my grandmother's home were obeyed and life on the surface was orderly and uncomplicated. Life underneath was okay too.

One day I was sitting right at the very front of Biology when Lucy Arnold knocked on the door. When invited to do so, she asked that I go to Mrs Woolcroft's office immediately.

Of course, the entire school was scared witless of Mrs Woolcroft, and I was no exception. Her black gown billowed through the corridors as free as her white hair was taut. Girls froze with straight backs hoping they weren't breaking an unknown rule as she passed.

I followed Lucy down these corridors, the oak panelled walls and parquet floors dimly reflecting the lights high above.

'Sit here,' she said as we arrived outside the office bearing Mrs Woolcroft's name. I'd never been this far down this corridor before. I'd only got as far as Mr Diamond's door and that was when he congratulated us for doing so well in the hockey tournament against St. Anne's.

It was lucky that I soon heard 'enter' because if it had been a long wait I might have become even more agitated. As it was when I tried to turn the brass door handle it slipped through my sweaty palm and I couldn't get a grip. I had to pull my cardigan over one hand and use the other to turn it. As I did I went from the darkness into light and had to squint.

When I found my sight again I was surprised to see my grandmother and grandfather sitting before her, Grandma upright with box bag on her knee, Grandpa hunched and avoiding my gaze. Sparrows before a hawk.

'Patricia Moore.'

I wasn't before royalty, and it was the 1980s not the 1950s, but I replied 'Yes Mam'. I'm not sure what came over me.

'Can you explain this?' Before her was a pile of white powder, and for a moment I had no idea how to explain it.

I looked at my grandparents, avoiding my gaze, and back at Mrs Woolcroft, eyes burning into my gaze, then at the white powder and then at the small floral bag sitting beside it. It was my washing powder.

I was embarrassed for them. I wondered what they thought their granddaughter was doing with the powder hidden at the back of her underwear drawer. (Along with that note Johnny Ashton sent me, I just remembered). I did think, for a moment: why did you look in my drawer? I felt the frustration of having nowhere, no place of my own. A small well of lava formed in my stomach.

But when I saw his head hanging low, I didn't feel betrayed. I pitied them. I saw how old they were, how helpless they might feel in this job thrust upon them.

'It's your washing powder,' I said. 'Smell it.' It was a type that my grandma bought, from Jacks. A surplus store, with big bags of washing powder. Barely a scent, not like the perfumed kind that my friends smelt of, but it was there. Why didn't she recognise it herself?

My grandma's body drooped, the rigid wrinkles dropped.

'It's just we'd heard the stories,' she was saying to Mrs Woolcroft. 'The ones in the Gazette, about the kids and the heroin and cocaine, even in the playground. We heard and we tried to ignore the stories. And then when we saw the bag it was all we could think of. And when I asked Mike Freeman, he said it was unusual for a girl of your age to spend so much time in her room.' She wasn't looking at me.

The pity was leaving my body. The well in my stomach began to swirl. She carried on, 'And the sneaking around the churchyard. Even Pru Richards noticed. She was the one who asked where you were. And we couldn't tell her.'

Mrs Woolcroft was nodding in affirmation. Grandma was feeling more understood. The lava was whirling and growing, in places burning my ribs. 'And when Angela Stanton said it was unusual for a girl to spend so much time running water in the bathroom, we really didn't know what to do.' The lava began to bubble, bursting and spitting as it travelled into my throat.

And then my headmistress said, 'There's nothing to worry about here, Mrs Moore. Our girls don't get involved in drugs. Now if you don't mind, we have lessons to be getting on with, and the piano concert with the boy's school band to prepare for.'

I watched her scurrying to stand. Heard his sigh of dissatisfaction.

I held open the heavy oak door, the brass sphere smooth in my grip. They passed through, him raising his brow, her looking straight ahead.

The lava settled and cooled. But a hard crust formed around the edges.

Suzie does as she pleases

The first time I saw Suzie we were both at Lou's drama group. I noticed her long dark pony tail and child's hair grip. I noticed the way she dressed – I liked it – and I noticed the holes at the tip of each foot revealing her big toes. I thought, how admirable not to care about exposing those big toes to the world. But then we were at Lou's *drama* group.

The second time I met her we were both at Jo's playgroup, the one at St. John's church. We talked. I said, 'Haven't I seen you at Lou's group?' I have used this approach to meet people before.

We go to St. Mary's on a Wednesday, and this was where I saw her next. I'll fill you in first. At St.Mary's group, there are chairs around the edge of the room for the adults, toys for the kids, a 'making' activity (supervised by kind volunteers – lovely), drinks and snacks for both kids *and* adults (unusual) and caring religious people to look after us all.

I'm not religious myself, but visiting these groups has helped me appreciate something. There is some good that comes from it.

For those feeling unsettled, abandoned, lost or alone (not me) there is comfort to be had at the church. If you don't mind pretending you'll come to a service once in a while.

Anyway, at this group there is a social division down the centre of the room. On one side there's us and the other side there's them. It's just come about, this social division, and it is an unspoken divide. But when I come in I always sit on one side and wouldn't dream of sitting on the other. For one thing, *they* never leave their seats, and *we* get up and down, swap around and pay our kids some attention. We get up for the singing, encouraging our little ones to be confident and not-at-all-self-conscious as we jump up and down to 'ring a roses'.

So this was the lay of the land when Suzie arrived.

It takes people a little while to pick their side, but they soon get what's going on. With Suzie, she sat on the opposite side first and I went to join her – I like to help the new ones feel welcome. I made the classic mistake of asking her little girl's name, and then tried not to appear puzzled when she said 'Theo'.

'Oh, I just thought because of the puff sleeves... (and the pink patent shoes and floral skirt) but yes, I try not to conform to typical gender stereotyping with their clothes either.' I look up and notice that my son is wearing blue and my daughter pink. I worried afterwards that I might have offended her. But I needn't have worried, it seems everyone just assumes Theo is a girl.

Since then I have had long discussions with Suzie at the groups, about the authorities' reactions to her ideas not to send Theo to school, and I've continued talking to her without looking alarmed as she breast feeds her four-year-old son who is dressed as a fairy.

At first I enjoyed her difference, loved it in fact. I thought she might use her daughter's old clothes for her son because she has no choice. And then she said, 'Well he chooses those things and why not let him have them while he's so young?' And I fully agreed. Although, inside, I questioned, just for a moment, whether I would actually go to Clarks and buy my son pink patent shoes.

And then I started to hear things and watch and wonder. I heard that the mums at her daughter's school gate have requested that she stop breast feeding in public. That she bought the little boy a Fifi bike and every time I see her, he looks more and more feminine. His golden curls are growing longer and longer, his hair accessories more ornate. People call him 'she' and she doesn't correct them.

I'm beginning to wonder. And I watch the others at the group. Some of them (on the other side) are the mothers from the school gate I find out. And they look at her and him. On my side they chat in a friendly way but some have started pointing out her son's bad behaviour (no worse than any other) and I look over at her and she's sitting alone, but I carry on chatting to the person I'm sitting with and try to avoid the uncomfortable feeling growing inside. When I look around again she has gone without saying goodbye and I feel a little sad and a little relieved, and it is this feeling of which I am ashamed.

*

The following week Suzie didn't show up. The old status quo prevailed and everyone was content. They smiled, they laughed, and the two sides even seemed to mingle. But I was uneasy, anxious. I looked at the door on several occasions, I played with my children and I participated in light conversation. I wondered if she'd come back. I wondered about how she must have felt. What it would have felt like if it were me.

When we arrived the next week after that, late, there was Suzie, sitting on the right side of the room. I sat down next to her. She said, 'I tried to get him interested in a policeman's outfit and he wasn't having any of it.'

'I'd never try and get either of mine into a police officer's outfit.'

We sat and talked, she fed and we talked, we had our photos taken (it was that time of year), and I didn't care about anyone else or what they thought.

.

Evening Shift

They walk down the High Street, the five of them following her. She is prancing, shimmying and flicking her mane of long straightened hair, and her bottom, from side to side.

This is the manager, Sadie, the one who employed Jess a few weeks before after a ten minute interview. Looking her up and down she'd said, 'I don't *do* formal interviews.' Then she'd said, 'Watch this.' And Jess watched a film warning of the dangers of dishonesty, and stealing from the 'team'. One simple mistake, greed out of control, and Jess could lose her job, family, friends and her home, like the desperate actor in the video. She sat on the worn office chair and gripped the edges of the seat, and when the film finished she looked at the numbers on the walls, searching the room for clues about what she might expect, until the door behind her swung open and Sadie, and her sugary scent, joined her with the paperwork.

*

Just to make sure that she understands not to steal, Jess is checked at the end of the night, at eleven, when she finishes unpacking boxes, tagging, hanging, cubing, scanning and replacing stock in the stockroom or on the shop floor. They line up, all of them, those that have been here fifteen years and herself, here a week now. Opening their bags for Sadie to review the contents.

The workers are all mums. Jess stands closer to the ones that talk to her like they are mums, although they are not like *her* mum. Jess's mum wouldn't work in a place like this. Since she came to stay she barely leaves the sofa. They all work the night shifts they say, as Jess does, to make some extra cash. They Ebay, Avon, do school dinners, to make some more. And then, they say and wink, there are the others. The rule enforcers. The whip crackers. The management.

There's Sadie, Evening Shift Manager, and Emma, 'watch out for her,' they whisper, 'she's plotting to take over when Sadie leaves.' Tonight, Emma comes and stands on the edge of their workstation, a station of tubs ready for unpacking, resting her head on one large hand and says, 'I ain't wearin' no uniform. They know what they can do if they try and make me,' with a big voice and a big smile. She saunters off, through the polished shop front and into the shabby back stairwell. Jess can't see that it is she that should win the lead role, there are others here working much harder, and faster, than Emma.

For that's what Sadie has, the lead role. When she joins the team she takes over the unpacking and the conversation with stories of her daughter, Serenity. 'Of course she's the fish in *The Fish called Wonder* performance. You should have seen her when she finished her dance. She only walked forward and curtseyed, blowing big fish kisses at the audience. It was hilarious. In the end Mr Smith pretended to catch her in a net, and removed her from the stage that way.'

Everyone listens, and laughs at the right moment.

'You know Mr Smith at St. Hilda's, right? Just wonderful. All the mums say it. And of course he just loves Serenity. I'm so glad she had him last year. No offence, Margaret, but St. Mark's just wasn't right for her. Do you know what he wrote in her school report? "Serenity will make a fine actress, so good she is at finding the limelight"! And then do you know what else he wrote? That she was, "A real presence in the classroom"!'

Jess smiles too, watching the pony tail popping up from one side of Sadie to the other as her manicured hands rip open bags, sorting the merchandise into piles for different hangers. Trousers, tops, children's. As she does so, she continues to talk, now about her compliant and doting partner, the one who prepares a chilled glass of wine for her for when she gets in from work.

The others whoop in feigned jealousy. But later, when she has gone, they voice their incredulity.

Jess whispers her first words to Margaret: 'Don't you want to go for the Manager's job?'

'Me? Nooo. You've got to be desperate to do that job,' she laughs. 'Loads more work for not much more money. Desperate or ambitious.' She nods towards Sadie, now checking delivery papers at the till, her beautifully painted face reflecting the blue of the screen.

*

It's too hot. The tights Jess wore under her jeans to protect her from the November wind are damp with sweat. There are two pregnant mothers on her team. One manages to reach the back stairs but vomits in the corner of the stairwell.

'Why doesn't she go home?' Jess whispers to Margaret as she stabs the tag through the thin material just above the 'Made with Love' label.

Margaret keeps her eyes on the bag she is tearing open, 'She won't get paid.'

Jess watches the sick lady, a bump on her belly, auburn hair scraped from her head, her skin as pale and tinged with green as the lights pouring down from above. She won't get paid.

'Twenty minutes. Time's not good enough!' Sadie's voice echoes from a speaker. Jess sees Margaret glance at the others.

'Do hanging,' she says to Jess. 'Small, medium, large hangers. Cubes with sizes,' she points at the cube trolley.

Hanging the clothes that are passed to her now, Jess puts her hangers in the empty tubs on the floor. 'WHO HAS PUT HANGERS IN TUBS?' She stops still. No-one answers for her.

'Me,' she says, barely able to spit her voice past her lips, 'I put them there. Why?'

'It's my pet hate – move them!' Sadie's words slam into her ear as though they have been boxed . She quickly moves the entangled mass of plastic onto the small space on the pile of tubs from which they are working.

'NO HANGERS ON TUBS!' Jess' chest pounds, the blood has risen to her face. Her forehead glistens like the tiled floor. The auburn haired girl grabs them and shoves them inside so they are unseen.

*

They follow Sadie to Vineyard Street where she zaps her car. Cherchunk. Jess expects her to be driving something flash, like her dad does, but she's not. It's big and silver, a Ford not a Merc. She leaves them there, Jess, Margaret, Emma and the ladies with the bumps, and one by one they find their vehicles on the High Street.

As Jess unlocks her bike and the late cold begins to suck on the damp tights, she thinks about Sadie and her pet hate and her glass of wine and the lights and the pregnant women. She heads down North Hill, avoiding the people spilling over the pavement onto the road outside Molly Malone's.

The cold air attacks her damp forehead and then her exposed hands. When she unlocks the front door and slips the key back on the front door hook, the warm smells of their earlier casserole engulf her. She sits for a while as her mind softens, staring at neat shadows of the spotless room.

*

When Sadie parks outside her maisonette she can see the lit window, and her stomach turns again, slowly. She unlocks the door and sees the cheap shoes on the mat. His cheap shoes, and then two pairs of stilettos, this time, sitting on *her* door mat. She takes off her trainers and creeps up the narrow staircase. As she reaches the top she halts as her lounge door opens and the lodger walks out, down the corridor towards her. He doesn't see her in the shadows, but she stares at the curled hair of his silhouette as it approaches.

The curled hair that she has to pick up from the kitchen floor, and pull from her shower tray.

He steps into the main bedroom, the one that used to be 'theirs'. From the front room she can hear high pitched voices and screams of laughter from her sofa.

She steps quickly, lightly, into the empty pink room, and bolts the door behind her. Photos of Serenity line the window sill that was once hers, along with a group shot of her friends in their Fish called Wonder orange fish hats, Serenity in the centre. In the morning, when she gets up at six for the day shift, Sadie will drive to her mother's, where her daughter lives for now, pick her up and take her to the nice school around the corner.

The Ring

Sadie, their old boss, left to become a midwife. Apparently you get paid to train nowadays. Good for her. Emma's in charge now, times have changed. Power shifted and a status quo has almost been reached.

Emma and Jess are the early staff that drag the tubs from the pallets when they arrive at the store. Jess prepares the stations for the other girls to work on when they arrive at seven.

Tonight, when she pulls a heavy metal trolley of cubes towards her, it veers off to the right, crushing her hand against the corner of a door frame. After the shock, nausea spreads quickly through her body, and there's a resurgence of pain at her knuckle.

Jess runs to the bathroom and douses it with cold water. It's not as bad as all that. But it looks quite impressive, bloody and swollen and worthy of a little sympathy.

When she's done preparing she's put on 'sets' for the night. Tailored clothes that come in pre-hung. She has to strip the plastic from each garment, tag and then cube it. Some people hate doing sets. Jess doesn't. She likes the chance to work alone, to not worry about the others' opinions of what she says.

She's been here a while now, but is learning new stuff as she goes along, snatching information here and there to make sense of the bigger picture. But she still can't work quickly enough. She rushes and sweats and uses every moment but doesn't manage to earn any praise.

Trying to think and tag at the same time is difficult; she can't do both, so she concentrates on the job. Jess can hear the girls laughing at the station, where they're preparing the other stock. She starts listening to their conversation, she can't help it, their voices are loud. They're talking about Robert Gatling, a pop star, who died only last night.

It's Jo and Nicky she can hear, they're related (Jo has just got Nicky the job here).

Emma, although stamping her authority effectively on most of the staff, is a little fearful of the two of them. She might do anything to have their support. The three are potentially a dangerous combination.

'That Robert Gatling off the TV got what he fuckin' deserved. I knew he was gay – you can tell by his name – *Gay*tling. Ha ha ha.'

'Yeah – why a man wants to stick his cock up another man's arse I'll never know. Not right is it?'

Emma's goading laugh pervades the building.

Jess's heart pounds the wall of her chest. 'Say something,' it hollers.

It could have been her, Nicky, who boasts about drinking a bottle of vodka every weekend. It could have been any of them. But it's not, it's a thirty-three-year- old man. A celebrity, but still, somebody's son, friend, lover, brother.

Jess carries on hiding tags under the arms of suits so that no one will be able to steal them. She says nothing.

There is a lot of work for her tonight, she's struggling to finish. When she's done she must take the rail up to the stockrooms. She's the only one that is supposed to leave early, at ten.

Emma ignores her. Jess thinks she's timing how long it will take her to finish. But she may just be ignoring her. So she has a very big rail, and not much time left before her shift is supposed to be over. Emma says Jess must take it up and put it away. It takes her until eleven. When she unlocks the door for Jess to leave, she says she must speed up.

Jess climbs on her bike and cycles fast through the town, avoiding the drunk people.

She lets herself in and the cushion of warm smells comforts her. Her children are upstairs sleeping. She can hear the murmur of the television and see the dim light of a lamp in the front room. Showing her mother her injury she says, 'Look'. She turns from the TV.

'I hope you didn't scratch your grandmother's ring.'

Jess says, 'A heavy trolley crushed my hand.'

'But did you scratch the ring?' She glances back at the television.

Jess stands in the doorway and thinks: all you care about is the bloody ring.

But she says, 'No, the ring isn't scratched.'

Christmas Hours

It's the end of November. They turned the Christmas lights on in town tonight. Jess has had a week off and come back to warm greetings from the people she now knows at work. She grins at Emma, and Emma grins back.

They work well together, Jess is fast now she knows what she's doing. They prepare the store for the other girls and are ready early tonight. Standing waiting for the lift to take her up to the stockrooms, she sees them spilling onto the shop floor.

'Did you see your hours for Boxing Day?' Lucy asks her.

'No – do you know what they are?'

'You're doing the same as Katie. Katie, what were your hours?'

'One 'til eight.' Katie replies as efficiently as she unwraps plastic packaging from a sparkly vest.

'Oh, OK. What are you doing?' Boxing Day. Not good for Michael and Ella but then I'll get away from Mother again.

'Ten 'til four-thirty.' Jess's friend looks disappointed.

'I thought we only had to do four hours. Didn't you want to do the morning?' The lift closes as she speaks.

Later, as they're standing around the work station, the two of them talk in whispers. 'We all have to work Christmas Eve as well.'

'What? Which hours?'

'Two 'til six.' Lucy holds up a small child's dress that says, 'I want you,' in silver lettering on the front.

'Oh dear. How can they? Might as well spend Christmas here.' Jess is tagging, Lucy and Nicky are hanging and cubing, Emma strips the clothes of their packaging.

Nicky takes over the conversation, Jess has become familiar with her too. The three new people aren't with them tonight, and Nicky is talking about one of them. 'Thank God Sam isn't here, with her powerful...ahem...scent.'

'What scent?' Jess asks.

'Haven't you noticed how much perfume she wears?' Nicky turns up her nose as she looks at her.

'No.' Jess hasn't noticed at all.

Their boss says, 'You've been standing too close to her, Nicky.'

'Yeah, it's when she passes me the leggings she doesn't want to hang.'

'She doesn't like doing that, does she?' Lucy is concentrating on her speed and doesn't realise that she has just colluded.

'No, she's always palming them off onto me.' Nicky continues on her subtle path of destruction.

'She's a quick learner. She's only been here a few weeks, it's taken me months to work out which clothes to avoid,' Jess says. Lucy laughs a little nervous laugh.

Emma listens, she doesn't join in, she is taking to her role as Manager mostly professionally. Someone has commented to Jess that she is doing really well considering how lazy she was before.

She checks the time and tells Emma that she is going to take a rail up to the stockroom; she gets it just right so she will finish at ten. When she exits the lift there is a new sign on the notice board:

Here at Fine we strive to meet our productivity targets, within a friendly and caring team environment.

She spins around the ladies' stockroom, spotting a t-shirt she might get for her uniform. Nicky and Jo are still talking about Sam as Jess darts from trousers (down low) to dresses (up high). Nicky is saying;

'Yeah, she picked this up and said she liked it, revolting isn't it?'

As she stuffs fluffy dressing gowns into over full cubicles, Jess hears her mutter, 'Can't stand her.' She doesn't bother listening for more. She wonders if that's how they spoke of her when she first arrived, but then she thinks, well they're not talking about the others, so maybe not. And then, is it the colour of her skin? And the homophobic comments come back, and she feels a wave of nausea sloshing against the wall of her stomach. But she doesn't know that for sure, maybe not, maybe they just don't like her.

*

She wears layer after layer to keep the ice cold away from her skin, but it still bites her face as she speeds home down North Hill. As she open the front door the home air hits her senses, smells of early dinner still pervading the atmosphere. When she's settled she tells her Mother that she's working Christmas Eve and Boxing Day.

'Leave,' she says, as she continues to stare at the television.

'No, I can't just leave.'

But Jess thinks: why can't I leave? When I started I thought, get a job, any job. Do you think that you are too good now to get any old job? Why should somebody else have to do that job and not you? But should I keep my job when I can leave, just because I feel lucky to be able to leave when the others can't?

It's always been okay for her anyway, because she knows it's not forever, her mother's not staying permanently. Just until her legs are better.

And then she remembers, 'Wait a minute, my contract is only until the thirty-first of December. They may not renew it.' They might ruin her kids' Christmas and then let her go. Good reason to resign.

'Phone that girl Emma and ask her if it will be renewed,' her Mother says, still staring at the TV.

So she does.

'Hi Emma. I just remembered that my contract ends on the thirty-first of this month. Do you know if it will be extended?'

'Is there a reason why you want to know?'

'No, could you find out this week for me, please?' If she leaves it a week it'll be too late for Jess to resign before Christmas.

They finish their call and her mother says, 'Take me to my room then. It's late. Too late. I think you should just resign, I need you here now.' Jess lifts her from her chair and takes her to the room by the front door, the one that is now hers.

Emma leaves it a week.

Boxing Day

By the time she arrives at one, the staff have given up trying to prevent the shop looking like a jumble sale. Women are still competitively scouring rails with one arm, the other already draped with bargains.

Jess gets her red sale t-shirt on in the staffroom and joins them on the shop floor. One of the day managers (rude, grumpy, avoids eye contact) tells her where to go. She has been given the job of getting the disregarded stock from the changing room and redistributing it to the area from which it came.

She says hasty hellos to her friends as she bumps into them. They are busy, the hours pass quickly.

At some time in the afternoon, after the store has closed, a call from upstairs turns out to be for her. Jess is requested in the office.

She knocks, purposefully assertively, on the door and when she hears a 'Come in'. She comes in. The Queen waits a while, finishing what she is doing before she swings her chair around to face her.

'Take a seat.' She's a little nervous and, just a little, excited. 'Emma has broken both her wrists while skating at Rollerworld. She won't be in for a while and I'd like to offer you her post.'

'Oh. Great. Oh. Sorry to hear that. Can I think about it?'

'We need you to start Tuesday. You're the only one that knows the delivery procedure.'

'Can I call you tomorrow and let you know? It's just, I need to discuss it with my mother.'

As she re-hangs and makes good the dishevelled rails, she thinks about what that new job might mean. But whatever she thinks she still has a sense of excitement, of pride, at having been asked. A promotion. To *Manager*. Sounds good. Better than *Assistant*. And then, eugh, two broken wrists.

She speeds down North Hill and keeps up the pace as she cycles along North Station Road towards Asda. She can't wait to tell someone.

She lets herself in.

Her mother is lying on the sofa with her legs in the air, resting them on a cushion.'I can't wait for you to finish that job – it's too much for me sending the kids to bed two nights a week what with my legs and everything. I need you here to help me.'

'Well,' Jess says, beaming, 'Guess what?' She has to be careful how she puts this. 'They're keeping me on and they've offered me a pay rise! More money! What do you think about that?!'

'It's not really going to make that much difference is it? And do you really want to be doing that awful job when you don't need to? I thought you were finishing.'

Jess shoulders drop.

'I don't think I want you to work on a Sunday evening – it's too much for me. Tell them you're leaving.'

*

If you think Jess should take the job, go to: *The Unbearable Challenge of Being Manager* next.
If you think she should tell them where to stick the job go to: *Ribbon* next.

Ribbon

A Cath Kidston pink, Jo Malone style, ribbon is weaved by a giant needle through the days of the week, binding them together day after day after day. The ribbon looks pretty, but it pulls tighter and tighter as the days go by, as they stretch into forever. Eventually it is so tight that even this thick, luxurious ribbon must snap, leaving the days of the week to fall apart into great black chasms. Michael is screaming – Jess wakes with a jolt.

When she called to tell the Queen that she couldn't take the manager's job, she told her that her contract was ending anyway. She should call by to hand in her locker key and staff discount card.

At first, Jess was quite relieved not to have to go to work, to have to go anywhere. And then that same old feeling came over her. Irritation, boredom, frustration. She must get a job. That will help her feel better. Only if she gets a job will she feel better. She must get a job.

Jess writes letters. She starts with well paid jobs and by the end she is writing to anybody. There's a recession on. It's hard for everyone – not just her. But if she keeps it up, keeps going, keeps writing, surely *surely* she can get a job. Any job.

Her mother says, 'Calm down. What's wrong with you? Are you ill? You are ill. You need to go to the doctor.'

She thinks, 'Leave me alone. I can't get away from you. I need a job. Then I can get away. I can't get a job. I must get a job. Maybe there's something wrong with me. Maybe I am ill. Maybe I should see a doctor.'

Jess's ill. She's depressed. She has to take pills. That's why she's been so irritable with her mother. That's why she feels like she HATES her. It says so on the websites about depression. Finally a solution.

Her children are happy. Very happy, giggly children. Emotionally intelligent, with no cares in the world. Their week is full. Gymnastics, drama, art, play-dough, friends. The children are getting bigger. They squabble. She gets them mostly everything at the moment, but gradually, little by little, they can do more for themselves. Delicious, crisp independence.

She listens while she sleeps and from the moment she wakes, she gets, carries, is balanced and fair. She thinks in every moment about their development: educational, emotional, creative – you know what it's like. She makes breakfast, clears up breakfast, makes lunch, clears up lunch, makes tea, clears up tea, and all the while, makes sure they are eating the fruit, veg and carbs and drinking water. They wear clean clothes and their nails are cut.

Her mother is miserable. Jess does everything for her too now, the poor woman can't move from the sofa.

Tired at the end of a squabbly day and night, she says, 'I can't cope with this much longer. I need to work and the children need to go to school.'

'I don't think you should get a job, I don't think you could cope with a job,' her mother says. 'You're ill. You are taking pills after all. Go back to the doctor. I'll come with you. You can take me in the car. I'm upset by all this too. I need to put forward my point of view. It's not easy living with someone with depression.'

When she's woken in the night, Jess is having the fitful dream of a number line with days of the week attached like teeth, or cuboid rubber fingers. It stretches as far as the eye can see.

After putting her son back in his bed, and kissing him and telling him she loves him, she jumps back in her own and her brain is alert with answers.

Only when those days of the week, stretching out as far as the eye can see are firmly taken a hold of, ordered back into line, and managed by Jess, will they bounce along independently and together, giggling when they bump and content on their journey.

The Unbearable Challenge of Being Manager

That first night as Manager, the Queen took Jess into her office. She showed her through the procedures and paperwork. As Jess left the office exhilarated by her new responsibility, her Ladyship had said, 'Oh, and remember Jess – there are no friends in management.'

Jess wrinkles her forehead. Maybe not for you, with your headmistress manner, she thinks. The girls have become my friends. I'll be better, motivate them – they'll even be more productive. She says, 'We'll see,' with a smile.

That night, Jess called everyone together for a team talk. The nerves pricked at her arms. When she started to speak, she wasn't sure it was her that spoke. She wasn't sure if she was at normal pitch, or too quiet. So she thrust out her voice and felt too loud.

They were all looking at her; a horseshoe of blank faces. Thinking: Why has she got the job? She's only been here five minutes. Why should she get it? Why should we listen to her?

But as she talked, she looked. She knew the ones she could trust. Lucy and Katie were listening and now smiling as they would have before.

But it's a few weeks in, and Jess knows what she's doing now. She puts Nicky and Jo on sets, and selects the other teams according to who she thinks works well together.

She had to finish the paperwork from the goods that have come in, and then joined Lucy and Ellen in menswear – they're unpacking the kids stock.

Jo comes up to give us some kids' coats and says, 'Fucking bitch,' under her breath. For a moment Jess thinks she might be talking about her. But she is already confirming the *bitchness* of Nicky to Laura, one of the new girls.

Unfortunately Jo's brother, also Nicky's husband, and Nicky, are not getting along and the two girls aren't seeing eye to eye over the whole business either.

Jess says, 'I don't think that's appropriate language, do you, Jo?'

Jo stares at her.

She stares back.

Jo turns on her heel and walks back to her rail. Jess is relieved and carries on unpacking, leading by example and speeding up the pace for the other girls.

The team performance reviews need doing. It's a good job she's had her eyes wide open here. For instance, she could only give Lucy a 'satisfactory'. Knowing what she knows about her, she knows she's not 100% committed to her job. And she knows that she doesn't always wear uniform, particularly on her feet.

Katie is going to have a disciplinary for all that time she has off sick. Jess told Nicky beforehand and she thought it was hilarious. They should think themselves lucky they've got work, she'd said. They could have been let go like all the others with end of December contracts.

When she finishes the paperwork in the office she comes down to do a check of the station. 'WHO HAS PUT CUBES ON THE FLOOR?'

'It was me,' says the new boy, Matt. 'I put them there. Why?'

'It's my pet hate – move them.' Matt does as he is told, straight away, and moves the cubes on top of the station, which is already set up for optimum efficiency.

'NO CUBES ON THE STATION!' He jumps, and the cubes spill like white lettered dice across the black tiled floor. As he scurries to pick them up, Jess is pleased that things are running smoothly, and can see that even when there is a blip, she can rectify things immediately.

The Queen *was* wrong, she's doing well. In fact, management hasn't changed a thing. If anything the girls are working hard for her and she's growing in confidence all the time. Tonight, for example, there she was telling them all about Ella's impression of a toad in her ballet production of Winnie in the Willows. They were in stitches. Jess was on a real roll.

Isn't it funny that as your confidence grows, your sense of humour grows too?

*

When Jess gets home, they row. A row viler than ever. And do you know what, it's because she's being more assertive.

Her mother doesn't like it. Not one bit. But that's tough, isn't it.

Look at what she's done. Got herself a good job in the middle of a recession, Manager at that. She's doing well – the girls obviously like her management style. Nicky even brought her a coffee in from Starbucks today.

Who knows? Maybe she'll be recognised, put on the fast track management scheme, head office, Philip Green's right hand woman. Fuck Philip Green, she'll *be* Philip Green. The possibilities are endless.

And her mother knows what she can do, doesn't she? Pack her bags. Jess has spoken to her sister and told her the way things are. It's about time she did her bit and looked after her mother.

Jess can manage by herself.

The Hide

When he went to feed the birds in his aviary that morning, Miles Webb gave those that remained more food than he normally would have. The aviary was behind his lodge, which had been built in the woodland to the west of the reservoir. Miles thought no-one knew about the aviary, which contained the birds from the eggs he had found when Maria had gone. He didn't know the name of the large ugly creatures that had emerged as chicks from those shells, but he hadn't seen another in all his time working at the reservoir.

Miles had a daily routine. Before Brian, the new manager, had even arrived at the visitors' centre, Miles had usually walked the circumference of the lake, checking the hides, the woods, and the plants, enjoying the opportunity to work alone. What he didn't know was that Brian often arrived earlier than he thought, and had investigated Miles' home, the aviary and surrounding woodland on many occasions.

This morning, Miles unlocked the first hide on his route and scanned the darkness for anything untoward. On finding nothing he strode to the left window, unhinged and opened the wooden flap and all being well, locked it again and proceeded to the flap on the right. This he continued until he had checked all flaps of

Montgomery hide. He made sure that the door was closed behind him and the latch secure and walked to the next.

The sharp wind did not hinder Miles' journey along the edge of the reservoir, and from one hide to another. To his right the gentle slopes of patchwork fields were haphazardly joined with almost invisible seams. He could see, just below the peak of the hill, the tip of the new centre. They were still building, still going ahead after all his protestations that the views, the birds, would not be the same as those from the old hides.

As he walked on to the William James hide, his favourite, he could see the abhorrent skeletal structure looming over the edge of the lake.

Inside he took his place on the low bench, unhinging, and gently opening the narrow window onto the world. He got up and stood back in the small dark room which was no bigger than two metres square. And again, mesmerised by the slit of beauty which was not unlike a painting in a fine art gallery, he felt the heart murmur that he had felt every day since they'd planned – well Maria had planned and he'd constructed – the hides, the woodland walk and the whole place in fact.

When he left the hide as he had found it, he looked up, as he always did, at the rust-tinged maple trees still illuminating the dull landscape.

Today, when he reached Wyke hide, he did not unlatch the door, he did not look for anything untoward, and he did not enter. Instead he made sure that he was silent on approach, treading lightly and carefully and pausing a few yards from the hide to listen. On hearing nothing he moved another step forward and twisted his body so that his ear rested against the crack of the door. Now all he could hear was muffled scratching. Miles smiled.

*

Anne Brown unlocked her office that morning and saw on the calendar above her desk one of the green site visit stickers. Wincham reservoir. She sighed and turned on her computer. The new Pmail diary popped up. She still hadn't adapted to using the latest technology.

The phone rang, before she had had a chance to get her coffee. She snatched the handset from the receiver. 'Anne Brown,' she said.

'Oh hello,' said a voice. 'I'm phoning about the housing.'

'I'm afraid there's a lot of housing.' Anne was going to have to speak to Debbie about stopping the public access to her direct line.

'Oh,' said the voice. 'I need a house near the school. We've been given one too far away.' For God's sake she thought. Not this again. The woman with the disabled son. 'Is that Mrs Wade?' She looked back to her computer and began to scroll her inbox.

'Yes it is,' said Mrs Wade.

'Then I have told you that the only plot available is 127. They were allocated early on and there is no chance now of changing.' All those black unread Pmail diary introductory messages and one from her friend Amanda.

'But I know the man they say got the house near the school, number 110, and he doesn't need it, not like we do.'

'Mrs Wade. The plots have been allocated. There isn't anything that can be done about it. Now if there's nothing else, I'm very busy.' She opened Amanda's message and went to get her coffee from the kitchen.

*

When Miles approached the visitor centre he saw the beige mini cooper in the car park. He thrust back his shoulders and made sure that his sweater was still tucked neatly into his jeans. He entered the shop-cum-cafe briskly, interrupting the intense chat that Brian was having with the woman from the council.

'Hello, Miles. This is Anne Brown – she's come to have a look around.' Miles knew very well what she was here for; Brian had, of course, warned him of the impending meeting and everything that it meant for them.

He looked her up and down, she did not fit here with her pointed red shoes; she wasn't a birder or a twitcher, or part of one of the families that sometimes came. Maria had said that it was good for children to get close to nature, to the birds. What would happen in the future if the families did not come now? But Miles could not care less about children or their families or the future any more. Not since she'd gone.

His mouth did not force a smile, but he nodded in Anne's direction and as she followed him out of the building he gazed only ahead. So he did not see Brian carefully removing the binoculars from the glass cabinet.

As they moved silently along the walkway, through the woods, Anne commented on the dens he had created from logs. 'Did you make them?' She said.

He grunted.

She thought that the attempts at a woodland campfire looked a bit scrappy. Hurrying along behind him, she noticed the small lakes surrounded by bent and bulging and torn net fencing. When they came out into the open and she saw the hills surrounding the reservoir, she found them to be threadbare. It was a shame about the hundreds of small trees they'd planted, but then they should have sought permission early on.

When they arrived at William James hide he opened the door, unlatched the windows and left her standing in the wooden box. When she scurried out after him, he said, 'Did you see? Did you see what you will be drowning with your plans?'

'I saw. I know. It's nice here. But not as nice as it will be.'

'I know what you're trying to do,' he said. 'You'll destroy everything.'

'No. We won't be destroying anything. We'll be improving.' They were at the second hide now and he did the same as he had in the first.

'Did you see?' He looked her in the eye, willing her to understand.

'Yes. And do you know what you'll be able to see from the new centre?' Miles knew it was no use.

'I know what you want to do, but I'm not moving.' They wanted his lodge, the home they'd created together, until the day Maria had left without a word. He turned and strode toward the final hide. This one was really going to show her.

Her stomach tightened and then catapulted her voice from her mouth. 'You have been offered a good deal, Mr Webb, the new houses are much to be desired and yours, plot 110, is in the best position.'

When he continued to ignore her she said, 'And you do know that there will be a site manager position available at the new school?' As she stumbled after him, she began to open her bag to get out the plans, but he just said, 'Puh'.

'Have any other house you like?' She was catching him up again. 'Mr Webb. You know that we cannot maintain the water levels as they are, that the water companies have taken enough already and what with the new housing, the further reduction in the levels will mean that many of your birds won't have the right environment to survive here anyway.'

He had already heard this argument. He knew by now that he would not convince her. And Brian admitting his fear of entrapment had certainly given him food for thought. Poor Brian.

How foolish he was. Miles had to purse his lips now to prevent a smile.

Anne was preoccupied by her fight, and the knotted fishing baskets piled against the side of the hide they had approached. Before she knew it, he had stopped and she walked into the back of him. She stepped quickly to his side, treading too heavily on one foot, losing her balance and grabbing one of the cages at the top of the pile for support. Fortunately they were heavy, and knitted together by the ends of the ridged ropes that formed the bars. She smoothed down her woollen coat and took a deep breath.

When he opened the door to Wyke hide she walked in voluntarily. When he slammed the door behind her she was momentarily startled. When the birds in their shock flapped and screeched and scratched she fell backwards trying to protect her face with her hands.

After what seemed like long enough, he opened the door and said, 'Do you see now?'

*

Anne cowered in the corner with her head wrapped in her arms. When he opened the door she shuffled towards the light. When he said, 'Do you see now?' and laughed, she inched down the slope veiling her eyes, and as she lowered her arms they felt heavy.

Her nose ached and her legs could not stretch from a squat. She felt the urge to push. The strength of her thrust was such that she propelled herself through the cold wind swooping into the sky as though she were swimming, sweeping back the water in giant breast strokes. Her arms were so powerful that she let her legs dangle behind her, delighting in their weightlessness. She swooped high. High up to the sky and then stopped.

She hovered. And she sang. The song swept through every inch of her; a sherbet tingling in her claws, a whirling hot lava in her rotund belly, shooting lightening forks to the tips of her wings. When it left her, the pinnacle of her experience was its perfect pitch.

Miles Webb stood outside Wyke hide as his precious birds escaped, squeaking and squawking and spluttering, and stared up at the creature that hovered above him. The moment of revenge had certainly created an unexpected result.

The creature sang. And then she dived. As fast as a diver from the top board she hurtled towards him. She saw his eyes, wide and wild, and then shielded by the crook of his elbow.

*

The local news said that the caretaker of the reservoir had been attacked by his own birds. Council worker Anne Rose Brown had disappeared on the very same day visiting the site. Although her red jacket and shoes and samples of her blood had been identified, no body had been found.

Neither had a close relative that could indicate their preferences otherwise so a memorial to them both would be placed in the new lake. The one that would flood the old, and become the centre of a new complex. A viewing tower would be ideally positioned for viewing the small island that would hold the memorial plaque, in the very same spot that Wyke hide now stood.

The lake would provide drinking water for the growing towns of Bide and Wincham, where a twenty per cent population growth was predicted and which would be accommodated by the many family homes to be built around the reservoir. And of course, the creation of which would provide jobs and educational experiences for the whole community.

*

But before they came to proceed with the next stage of the expansion works the council were forced to stop. A rare bird, then another and then a third, as yet unidentified, had been spotted.

They perched on the top of Wyke hide and swooped back and forth between the maple trees. They had been observed for a while and rarely sung, but when they did their song was almost melancholic.

And then, some others, blue-necked and at once beautiful and grotesque, were seen trotting across the fields as if they had been there all their lives.

Rare bird alerts began popping up on all the best websites. Of course, the twitchers started arriving in droves and the café was full for the first time. Brian was so pleased with his letter to the council and its effects that he wrote the new job description for the caretaker too. He went into the woods and started to remove Miles Webb's attempts at forestry and to rebuild the woodland camps. Then he called his friend Alice who was head of the local Scouts group (and someone he was rather keen on) and arranged that they come and recreate the woodland walk. He gleefully released the last birds from Miles' private aviary and decided, that after a lick of paint, he would move into the woodland lodge himself.

The Short Story

The woman stepped slowly out of the mobile home. She and her family had stayed there, for the first time, the night before. She broached the fresh air and wondered if she would be wearing the right clothes for the weather. But the mild breeze that enveloped her exposed skin was a good match and she carried on dressed as she was.

She'd heard their voices from inside the caravan. Her husband was talking to someone, a man. As she approached them and then stood by his side, he continued to speak to her husband without looking at her. Then her husband said, 'This is my wife.'

He said, 'Hi,' and continued the conversation as though she was not there.

The man was talking about a fire that had taken place on the camp site a few days before, when they were woken by shouts of, 'Feu, feu!' and leapt from their beds at five o'clock.

Her heart expanded, swelling so that she knew it was there, as her head reconsidered the acceptability of her surroundings.

As he spoke, his partner, who had very long, very straight, blonde hair and what looked like ironed shorts, came out of their tent, nodded at her and put some food on their table.

She stood where she was, and wondered if the man would make eye contact with her again, but he did not. As he spoke she thought she'd heard his type of voice before. Later on, she recalled that it was a mixture of people she recognised in him, coincidently all involved in education.

As she cleared the dishes from breakfast, she thought about a story she'd just read by Fay Weldon.

At the time she'd found it quite irritating to read about the everyday activities that the protagonist has to do as a parent, or more specifically as a mother. The descriptions of the anxiety of thinking about every meal and being responsible for planning for it, so that the inevitable pain to the senses of children being hungry and whiney does not occur.

She now thought how accurate it was. And how, although she had once been a strong independent feminist, ever since she had had children she had become that woman. Maybe that story is pretty good after all.

But that's not the story I want to write, she thought, because she was trying to be a writer herself. I want to write a story that has a strong female role model for my daughter. After all, that's what stories are for, for learning from, she thought.

Had she not had a daughter, or a son, she never would have presumed to teach through storytelling, but now she felt it was her obligation, her duty, to do something good, great even, to show her children that she was not only a mother, but an intelligent person and one from whom they might learn some of the answers. Because the woman also knew that if you just try and tell your children, or *anyone*, what to do, then they might just not do it.

This is what she thought as she stood thinking about herself, standing at the sink in the caravan.

Her husband brought in the rest of the dishes and washed up the rest of the things.

She opened the book that she bought in the service station on the way to the ferry, *How to be a Woman* by Caitlin Moran. It was, you know, funny and tongue-in-cheek, but she thought she might get some ideas for a message for her story.

The children charged out of their bedroom with their plastic swords raised and ran down the steps and outside and she put the book down again quickly, and did her job, which was to watch them and make sure that they were okay, that no one took them away. That they had good and fun things to do so they didn't get bored and squabbly, that they ate at the right time so they didn't get unnecessarily whiney.

The children were charged with the energy of the new holiday home.

'Can we go to the park with the elephant slide?' they squealed.

'Wait one minute while I get my book.'

So while the children played on the elephant slide, she sat on the blue bench and read the book and thought about the author's life experiences and her messages about how to live now. Her husband came along and joined in with a game of table tennis, and she thought that it was good that she got a bit more time to read her book.

Every time they left the caravan she remembered to take her book. At the end of the second day the husband wanted to sit outside and have some adult conversation he said, but she said that she was too tired and wanted to read her book.

He said, 'That's what families do.'

And she said, 'don't tell me what families do, we make out own rules,' and got into bed and they'd had their first holiday argument.

She sat there and she felt pleased that she'd answered him back instead of feeling guilty and sitting outside like she once might have done. But then he got into the bed too and she couldn't concentrate on reading while he angrily pretended to go to sleep next to her.

On the third day, she lay in bed and her husband went to the shop and bought croissants, *pain au chocolat* and bread. He made her a cup of tea and brought it to her in bed, and she knew that he'd listened to what she'd said and was making it up to her.

She got up and went outside wearing a long cardigan over her pyjamas. She sat with the children and her husband, and felt that her body was light. This is why people go on holiday.

She thought of her own thoughts of yesterday, about the Fay Weldon story, and she thought, no that is not me – that was only a moment of thinking it – of course it is not me. I'm more relaxed than that woman. I could be the second woman in the story, the easy going, relaxed one. I mustn't take the things my husband does for granted.

So they went to the beach and she took her book and she read through the life of Caitlin Moran, the author, and she noted down one of the main ideas she was interested in.

Sexism has become more subtle. No longer is it as overt as it once was. It has become covert. Yes – that's true, she thought – subtlety. That's what I've been stuck on. There is behaviour that is there that you can feel uncomfortable about and yet you cannot say, 'How sexist!' as we once could, because it is more subtle now.

So she wrote it down in her notebook. Then she wrote a description of the beach and about the man who had spoken to her husband, his wife with the long blond hair and the bits of his fire story that she had heard.

That afternoon, after lunch of bread and ham and Saint Nectaire, she got the Scrabble from the camp site supplies. They began to play and almost immediately her husband said to their son that it was boring, and that Mummy just wanted to win all the time. She thought this was ridiculous, because she had never felt like she wanted to win in a game against the children, ever. And she said so.

That night at bed-time the children got into their bunks and the woman wanted to read her book. Her husband said that he wanted to play Scrabble. She said, 'I thought you didn't want to play Scrabble. I thought you didn't like it.'

He said, 'I just didn't think I could make any good words. But, maybe it is something we could play together?'

She felt sorry that he wanted to play because he thought she would play with him. So they played Scrabble until their eyes were red and sore and they filled the board with words and both enjoyed it.

In the morning, once again she was in bed when he went to get the croissants and the *pain au chocolat*. They sat under the umbrella and appreciated the sun and the outdoors, and the people walking past in their dressing gowns to go to the showers.

As they ate, a little girl came and stood next to the children in silence. There she just stood. The children became animated and excitable and so did the woman.

'Hello, what's your name?' She said to the little girl. Soon a little boy arrived too. They were the next door neighbours.

The children started to speak to each other and tentatively they went from caravan to tent exploring the others' accommodation and excited to have someone to show.

Both sets of parents made sure that they could see what was going on and were ready to step in should any behaviour of their own children become unreasonable.

The woman watched the other parents as they passed by, and they began to say hello to one another.

The oldest child from the other family, who liked to talk, was engaged in conversation and soon she was offering to walk with them all when they asked to go to the fitness playground. After some demonstrations of the equipment the second mum arrived and the first was pleased and eagerly found out all about her.

'Have you been at the camp site long?'

'Have you been to this one before?'

'Which ferry crossing?'

'Where from?'

'Edinburgh! Lovely – such a long way though.'

'Oh yes, a very good idea to break the trip.'

'We've thought about getting our own caravan next year.'

'Oh yes I know, they *do* have that image don't they. It's just, we have the long summer holidays.'

'Yes we are both teachers. We're lucky. What about you, what do you do?'

Cautiously they all made friends and she read her book less.

In the evening the children played out late and the parents stayed up late. The next night, the night before the new friends were due to leave, they all joined together and stayed up until the children brought themselves back to the tent to settle down.

The following day there was an emptiness about their part of the camp site.

The woman wrote down about the new friends in her notebook, and wondered if their promises to book the same destination again next year would come to fruition. Probably not, she thought despondently. Holiday friendships, all very exciting at the time but don't really come to anything.

They waited with anticipation for the next family to arrive – having found the wonders of holiday friendships and thinking that they were easy. But the next family refused to make eye contact, even when they sat outside their caravan, broadly smiling and trying to say, 'Hello'.

The woman wrote about the disappointment and then finished reading her book about how to be a woman.

The next day she wrote a short story.

A man took his family to France for a holiday which they all needed, and was well deserved. He had broken up from an exhausting summer term of disputes and outdoor pursuits and exams and management meetings. To top it all, they had just had an OFSTED inspection. The school had received an outstanding report which was obviously down to his management style, and a deputy who made sure that they were always on top of the latest developments in education. She was a credit to the team.

His wife had arranged the holiday and he hoped that she had booked a good camp site this year. Of course, now he was a Head they could afford to have the pre-made tents. She had wanted to try one of the mobile homes instead, but he had said, 'No. We're not a caravan family.'

The man drove the car and got cross with his wife when she made small mistakes – this didn't happen very often because she had fine-tuned her map reading so that she received as little criticism as possible, and actually she was very good at it.

When they had been in their tent only a few days they were startled to hear the cries of 'Feu! Feu!' and the rasping of shoes on the gravel.

The man and woman leapt up and out of the tent and the man shouted, 'Get the children!' The woman dragged the children out of their sleeping bags, and out of the tent.

Once they were all safely outside, the man stood in front of his family and the family peered out to see what was going on.

The woman, from where she was standing, behind the man, could see through a gap in the hedge to where a small boy was turning a knob on the top of one of the gas canisters. Before the man could stop her she shouted, 'Arrête!' and ran towards the boy, who turned toward the shout, and then ran backwards into another hedge behind the caravan. In French she shouted, 'Stop that boy!' She picked up her shoe and flung it at his head. She took off the other and flung it into the bush where he had disappeared. She turned the dial of the gas canister so that the gas stopped escaping. And she picked up the box of matches which lay by the side of the canister. The husband shouted, 'Stop that boy!' as she had, but couldn't find him when he searched.

When the camp site owners came to ask them what had happened, the husband, who could not really disassociate his work persona from his life persona, stood in front of his wife and said, 'There were some boys that were fiddling with the gas canisters – of course I tried to catch them, but they got away.'

The owners said that they had kicked some boys off the camp site earlier in the week for not obeying the ten o'clock noise curfew. They thanked him for his assistance and went to watch the fire fighters who had just arrived, an hour after they were called. They were dealing with the remains of the camp site tractor, which was thankfully the only victim of the incident.

After all that excitement, they sat down to breakfast which he had just bought from the shop.

Later, the wife brushed her long hair a hundred times, and then her daughters' long hair a hundred times. When the new visitors arrived at the camp site, the husband went to tell them all about the adventure, while she made dinner. She listened to him talk through the window of the tent while she cooked the green beans and garlic.

Then, she turned off the gas, for the second time that day.

She looked at the map, wrote down the main motorway numbers, picked up the car keys, and drove herself through France alone. At the port she boarded the next ferry back to England.

The husband asked if he could read her story. When she read it out to him he said, after a moment of silence and while she looked at his face in anticipation, that it was a bit boring. That it didn't really have a plot or a beginning, middle or an end. Not really much description of place or character, and not much action either. Then he said, 'And why does she go?'

'Because she's angry,' the woman says.

'Why is she angry?'

'Because her husband, although he preaches about equality, and *should* do in his job, does not treat his wife equally, or fairly.'

'He's not preaching about it.'

'No, but it's the way he acts.'

'So why doesn't she say something? Why doesn't she tell him that is what she thinks?'

'Because he won't listen. He's too full of his own self-importance. It's in every inch of him.'

She got up and put the kettle on the stove.

'Actually, maybe I'm not that good at writing stories after all. Maybe that is not the story I wanted to write, or the message I should give.'

She thought about the message: strong woman, subtle sexism. She thought; strong woman, subtle sexism. I'm not sure that I really need to write a story about that to give my daughters and sons a good message about how to live.

She thought about her holiday and the changes that she and her husband had struggled to make in their own marriage, how they argued more and yet she was now saying exactly what she thought. She knew that it was not as simple as picking up the car keys.

I don't really need to write a story to show them how to be, she said to herself. I just need to show them how to be.

*

When the woman got home she thought: I'm going to send that story off to some magazines anyway. Maybe *someone* will like it. It is rather funny after all.

She could not believe it when, not long after it was sent, she received an email from *Made-Up* magazine telling her that her story would be published in the September issue. They were doing a short story special.

She waited patiently for the magazine to come out, and every day she checked in the Post Office to see if it had arrived.

When it did, she picked it up almost desperately and opened each page until she found the one where her story was printed. Next to the article was a watercolour of a woman combing her long golden hair. And there they were, her opening words! Her own words. In a magazine. She picked up five copies and could not conceal a smile as she purchased them. She wanted to say to the lady behind the counter, 'I have a story published in this magazine! I'm an author!' But she didn't.

She texted her husband and he brought home some champagne and when the kids were in bed they looked at it together. When she began to read, the story felt different. By the end the woman was travelling back to England, not alone, as she had written in the original story, but with a honey-coloured stranger.

She ran to get a copy of the story she'd sent and then read it alongside the one in the magazine. The description of the man's work had gone, the fact that he was a head teacher had been removed. When the new visitors arrived, instead of cooking dinner, the wife went to watch the fire fighters in action.

While watching the 'brave, muscular and attentive' men at work she decided that enough was enough with her 'cowardly fella', and drove off into the sunset with someone far more suitable.

Her body had felt a natural elation, which had fizzed to a peak when she began to read what she thought were her words, her name. As she realised what had been done, the deflation was as extreme and she could not contain her anger as she cried, 'Look what they've done – that's not what the story was about! That's not what I wanted to say!'

Her husband said, 'Calm down. Does it really make a difference? You've been published. In a magazine. Does it matter that they changed the story a little?'

'Of course it matters! I wanted to show the build up of the way he behaves means that eventually, after a long time of putting up with it, she just calmly picks up the car key and leaves. Not that she's just bored and is saved from one rubbish bloke by another! And do you think I want people to think that my protagonist would leave her children on a whim – for a –' she nearly chokes, 'handsome fucking stranger?'

'It's just a silly story in a magazine. No-one reads those things. Especially the short stories. Anyway, there's not much you can do about it now,' he says, and switches on the television.

'Yes there is.'

She goes about writing an angry email to the editorial department and another to the letters page.

All month she checks her emails waiting for a response but she does not receive one.

When the October issue of *Made-Up* comes out and arrives at the Post Office, she grabs a copy and turns quickly to the letters page. Scanning it she does not see her own words, but her eye rests upon the title of her story in another letter. And then another.

'I liked your story, it reminded me of me and my husband. But when I took the car and drove off in it he phoned the police and said that it had been stolen. When they found us he acted all

surprised and full of pity and said that I need some help with my problem. Margaret, Kent.'

'I absolutely adored the story 'Being a Woman'. I decided that I would leave my awful husband for the gardener after all – good for me! Jill, Warrington.'

The woman stood in the Post Office and wondered about writing stories with messages, and editors of magazines, and felt full of despair.

The next day, she got up and the sun was spilling through their bedroom window, its white-yellow glow permeating the space, and her mind. Its warmth cushioned her face; her arms; her exposed skin.

She said, 'Right. I'll show them.'

Room 15

Michael lay down on the velour sofa and after plumping the lurid red cushion, closed his eyes. He was safe in the knowledge that if a hotel customer rang the bell, the door to the basement was locked and he would have plenty of time to compose himself before going up to see them.

When he first started the reception job, he had diligently carried out the tasks he had been asked to do: checking the diary for expected guests; letting in the new arrivals; showing them to their rooms. Refilling the tea, coffee and milk in the rooms soon to be accommodating new guests; refilling the cornflakes packets in the breakfast room with the cheap version that they replaced. Dusting. Now, he always made sure he checked the diary. But as it became more and more apparent that no one was ever going to come and check up on him, or come down the stairs without him at least knowing about it in advance, he did fewer and fewer of the jobs he found he could get away without doing. Dusting, for example. And, if when he checked the diary, no one was due to arrive, sometimes, quite often now in fact, he even pretended he hadn't heard the bell when it rang. It would only be someone asking for an iron, or a hair dryer, and to be honest, he thought that they should manage to go without either for a weekend break.

It was the rattling chandelier that woke him this evening. He stared at a small crack above his head, on the edge of an ornate ceiling rose. Skimming the circumference, he saw a thin grey vein on the other side. He hadn't noticed it before. Holding his thumb in the air above him, he measured its length.

The rattling stopped.

Michael shut his eyes again. The noise began again in earnest until it became more of a shake. This nap was not going to happen. He would eat some fake cornflakes and watch Coronation Street. He pulled his heavy head up slowly; the sluggish tiredness was developing into a headache. As he gently pressed his temples he noticed a shard of white plaster on the cream carpet. Stooping to look closer and then turning to gaze up at the crack, he was showered with a fine dust which powdered his face and, more unfortunately, fell straight into both eyes. He screwed them tight and pummelled them with his knuckles, so he didn't notice the shake intensifying into more of a quake; the chandelier clearly swaying from side to side and the crack spreading what would have been a good inch if he'd measured it again with his thumb.

He rubbed more vigorously, only focussing on the inside of his eyes: the blood that must surely be filling the whites of them; the raw scratches which must surely be etching all surfaces; the searing pain binding what must have become incisions, into one big, roughly woven canvas now covering both eyes and merging itself into the headache and becoming more and more tightly knit all the time, eventually piling itself up and coming to rest in a deep bloody mound above his right eye.

As this took place, he sat directly beneath the crack which had, in the space of seconds, become a chasm and through which plunged the heavy oak four-poster from Room 15.

On top of the bed were Mary and Bob, who, because Mary could not go out wearing a crumpled dress, and because Bob had forgotten their travel iron, and because earlier when Bob rang the bell at reception to try and enquire as to whether they might be able to borrow one ('Surely they will have one, Bob. Which hotel doesn't have an iron?') and no-one answered ('Are you sure, Bob? Did you press it properly?') they had decided after frustration and tears not to go out that evening, to call it a day and wait until tomorrow to make their special romantic début into the posh town they were visiting.

Eventually they made up. Bob had popped out and got supplies: Typhoo for the morning; Mary's favourite bottle of Pinot Grigio Blush and a Domino's pizza (Bob's favourite – American Hot – Mary just picked at it), and had had quite a romantic evening after all.